T R E A S U R E

WARNER BOOKS

A Warner Communications Company

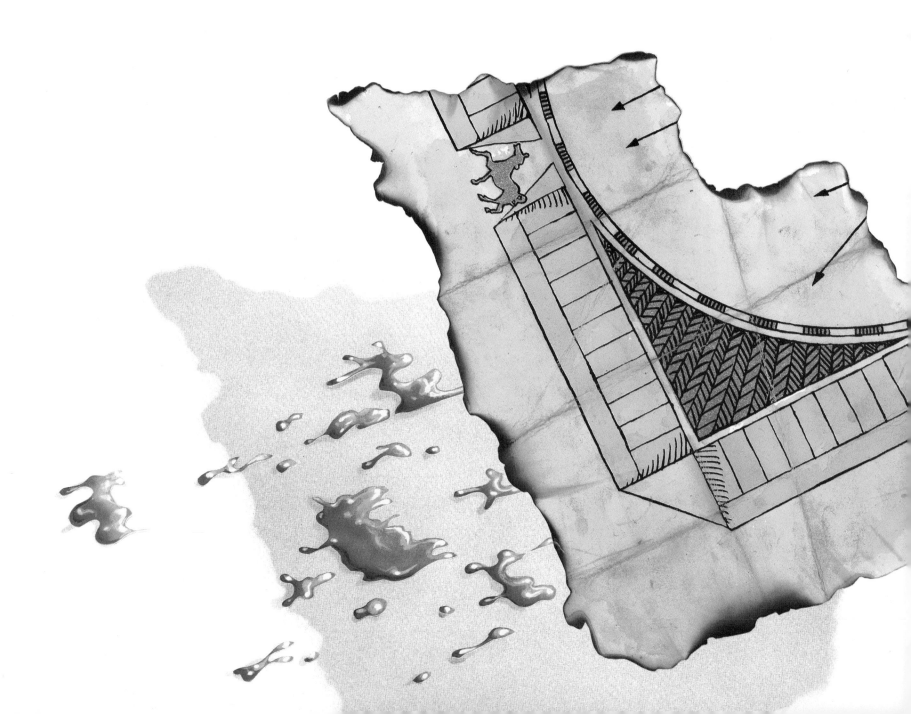

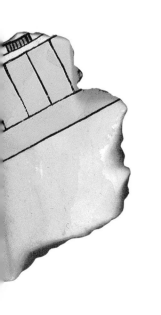

Somewhere in the earth is buried a horse of gold.

Buried in this story are the clues that will lead you to that secret place.

Find, link and follow the clues that lay hidden in this tale, and you will come to understand the map...

For it shows you exactly where to dig.

But do not dig too deep.
Break no law. Take no risk.
It is in a safe place.

And when you find it, look into the heart of the golden horse, for there hides the key to a great fortune...

Waiting for you.

This book is for Ingrid, Lisa and George...for Kira...for Jordan Frances...for William...for Joshua and Jordan Rush...for Troy, Blake, Yoshio, Kenzo, Nobu and Mark...and for Paul's children when they come.

With thanks...To Peter Bloch, who supervised the production. To Rory Nugent, creative supervisor for IntraVision, for his help under difficult conditions. To Jim Frost, a truly creative editor, for his many excellent suggestions. To Laurie Handler of COY, Los Angeles. To Dr. Crypton, wherever you are. And above all, to Barry Grieff, Jon Grossman, and Herb Nagourney who made it all possible.
—S.R., Los Angeles, April 1984

TREASURE

In Search of the Golden Horse

A Puzzle by Dr. Crypton

A Fairy Tale by Sheldon Renan
Based on a Story by Sheldon Renan and J. David Wyles

Illustrations by Jean-François Podevin

Book design by COY

An IntraVision Book

Warner Books Edition

Copyright © 1984 by IntraVision, Inc.

All rights reserved.

This Warner Books edition is published by arrangement with IntraVision, Inc., 18 East 53rd Street, New York, NY 10022

Warner Books, Inc., 666 Fifth Avenue, New York, NY 10103

Ⓦ A Warner Communications Company

Printed in the United States of America

First printing: September 1984
10 9 8 7 6 5 4 3 2 1

Library of Congress Cataloging in Publication Data

Crypton, Dr.
   Treasure.

   "A fairy tale by Sheldon Renan. Based on a story by
Sheldon Renan and J. David Wyles."
   "An IntraVision book."
   1. Literary recreations. 2. Puzzles. 3. Treasure-
trove. I. Renan, Sheldon, 1941-   . II. Title.
GV1493.C78 1984   793.73   83-40524
ISBN 0-446-38160-8 [pbk.] [U.S.A.]
       0-446-38161-6 [pbk.] [Canada]

Maps on page 42 © Rand McNally & Company

CONTENTS

CHAPTER ONE

CREATION

Treasure was the name of the stallion.

He had a shining chestnut coat, a finely chiseled head, and a fiery spirit. Amanda loved him more than anything else in the world.

Seven thousand years ago his ancestors had crossed the steppes of Asia to the deserts of Araby. They had survived because they were fast, intelligent, and had limitless heart. This was Treasure's legacy. He too was pure and strong. And wild as the wind.

When the blacksmith saw the mighty stallion, he knew at once it was meant as a gift for his young daughter. But it was a gift too early given.

Amanda was only six, but already she was filled with light and grace and a fierce pride and love for her father. She had sparkling green eyes and long brown hair that always flew around her as she ran. She loved Treasure from the first moment, but she also feared him. He was too tall, his stride too long, his speed too great. And when he galloped across the pastures, the earth shook beneath his huge hoofs.

Her father tried to teach her not to be afraid. Every morning he would capture and bridle Treasure. Then, while the stallion waited in the meadow, his nostrils blowing steam, the blacksmith would lift his daughter high onto the horse's back. Together the three of them would walk: Treasure, Amanda, and her father. Treasure was so spirited and she was so young that she could only stay on the stallion with the help of her father's strong hands. But as they walked the fields and forests, Amanda felt the powerful horse beneath her and dreamt of the day she could ride him herself. She dreamt of being a princess and a huntress, of riding like the wind. She and Treasure...together they would go everywhere.

When the blacksmith saw the yearning in his little girl's eyes, he decided to give her another horse. But this horse would be gentle and easy for his daughter to hold. This horse he would make with his own hands. And he would make it all of gold.

It would be a figure with flying mane and tail, neck arching, hoofs pawing. It would be a horse that might have lived seven thousand years ago. A horse fit for a princess, precious as the dream his daughter carried in her heart.

That day the blacksmith began to sculpt a familiar shape from warm wax. He did it over and over, until finally it mirrored the power of Treasure's legs, the pride of his head, and the joy of his heart.

Hidden beneath the floorboards of the blacksmith's shop were precious metals that he had mined himself from the mountains beyond the forest. Many years had passed since he had placed the glittering ores there, but now he removed the purest nuggets from the secret cache. He heated the gold until it was liquid and could take the shape of dreams. Then he poured it flaming into a mold of wax and sand.

When the mold had cooled, the blacksmith dug deep into the black sand. His fingers found a tiny prancing leg, then a smoothly muscled body. He pulled the sculpture up into the light and brushed away the clinging sand. There in perfect miniature and cast of gleaming gold was her Treasure.

He set the horse to cool by the window and looked out toward the pasture where, safe behind a split-rail fence, his daughter watched her stallion graze. The blacksmith imagined the moment when she would first set eyes on the golden horse. She would smile and ask who it was for and he would tell her.

"It's for you."

11

CHAPTER TWO

THE MAN WITH BLACK GLOVES

I n her bed that night Amanda waited for her father to come and put out the light. She didn't want to go to sleep until he had kissed her good-night. *I'll just close my eyes for a moment,* she thought, and drifted off to sleep.

In the moonlight her stallion stamped his hoofs in anticipation. Amanda swung easily up onto his broad back, and when Treasure reared and started to run she took firm hold of his mane. She felt as strong as he.

Faster and faster they went, galloping across the pasture to the edge of the dark forest, and through the forest to the sea, with its dangerous waves and blowing surf. But she was carried high and safe by Treasure's mighty legs. Together they raced the moonlight and drank the wind.

Treasure leapt into the air and carried her higher and higher. And the moon turned him the color of gold.

All the while, beneath Amanda's room, her father sat by the hearth and polished her gift. It was a special gift that held a secret within. For in the belly of the horse, through a cleverly hinged door, her father had slipped a key. And in her sleep the young girl frowned and wondered, *What does the key unlock?*

Her father came into her room and pulled the quilt over his sleeping daughter. It had slipped from her bed as she had raced along the waves, leaving

her cold in the wet sea wind. Gently he pressed his lips to her forehead, then doused the light and left the room. But he did not leave her alone. On the table by her bed stood the beautiful golden horse, gleaming in the moonlight.

Suddenly the wind blew strong and cold. The trees groaned, and Treasure neighed a warning in the night. Amanda tried with all her strength to open her eyes, but storm clouds crossed the moon and pressed heavily against her lids. Darkness now entered the house. It made no sound, yet she could feel its every step. Though the door did not move, she felt it come into her room, and she could see . . .

The Man with Black Gloves.

His darkness closed around the golden horse, and in that moment Treasure vanished from her sight. "No! No!" she cried, but thunder drowned her out. The black gloves turned into a great black bird that flapped its wings once, then flew away with the storm.

The cry of a hawk awoke her. The morning sun shone clear and bright outside her window. But Amanda sensed something was wrong. Her heart beating fiercely, she hurried to the stable. It was empty. Treasure was gone.

Bewildered and afraid, Amanda ran to find her father. She searched the house and the workshop and all the nearby pastures. But she never found him. Like Treasure, her father had disappeared in the storm. And with him went all that was precious in her life.

15

KITES

"G o," she ordered the kite. "Find my Treasure."

For Amanda, kites were alive. She felt their pulse through the string in her hands. She saw their life as they caught the wind and rose with it, bobbing and straining to be free.

Unlike the kites, she was trapped on the ground. She was alone now, or as good as alone, for Aunt Margaret was more custodian of the farm than companion. Since she had arrived to take care of Amanda and manage the estate, she had spoken only once of Amanda's father, and that was only to stop Amanda from asking questions about his disappearance. *She* would not help search for the missing stallion, and so Amanda sent the kite instead.

It was her favorite kite, the one she had painted blue like the sky, with a golden horse that pawed the air with his hoofs as Treasure had. She hoped its paper eyes would find her horse of flesh and breath. Each spring morning, she sent the kite aloft. And each time it returned to earth...without a clue to her Treasure.

One day a storm came up without warning. A squall of clouds and a scissor of wind snapped the thin string, and the kite flew off...perhaps to join her horse.

Each year she made new kites to fly high, to escape, to find her missing stallion. There were big kites and small. Kites common and kites strange. Kites

with fish and frogs. Kites with birds and the things they eat.

Twelve springs (and twelve kites) passed without success. On the first day of the thirteenth spring, she painted a new kite and made it exactly like the first kite the storm had taken. But now she was older, her hands were stronger and wiser, and no gust of wind could break this string or take her kite away.

"Go. Find my Treasure," she ordered the kite, as she had each and every kite before it.

The wind took the kite higher and farther than ever before. The wind went everywhere there was to go and saw everything there was to see. This time, when the kite returned, it rustled and crooned in a magical voice. And Amanda heard it say:

> "To find your Treasure
> you first must find
> your father's grave."

19

CHAPTER FOUR

CEMETERY

othing Aunt Margaret told her revealed how her father died or where he was buried. In Amanda's eighteenth year, her aunt left the farm, telling her that she was no longer a little girl in need of care. It was true. She could take care of herself. She had her inheritance and could travel. She would search the cemeteries that lay hidden among the hills of her childhood. She would keep trying until she found him.

The cemeteries were places surrounded by silence, but Amanda did not find them peaceful. Although she knew it was time to take the first step toward finding her father, she felt unsettled. First steps can be very painful.

On the eighth day of her search she found a cemetery that was older and odder than any she had seen before. A corona of clouds spread above it, and a line of trees encircled it. Between the clouds and the trees soared a large black bird, unnaturally shaped and making an unpleasant cawing sound.

A chain of curious links was carved atop the archway of the cemetery gate. Each was a different shape and each a different color. Amanda stopped to stare. It was almost as if there were a warning in the air. How hard Amanda found it to cross this portal.

Once inside the cemetery gate, she found a landscape of stones, markers of

20

death in many shapes and sizes. Some graves had a few names, and others just one. Three times she found stones with names worn away. Many stones were carved with messages of sorrow and love, but now cobwebs connected them all and lizards played among them. Old flowers rustled in a dry wind. Amanda had brought a single red rose to lay on her father's resting place. As she walked from stone to stone, reading the names and messages inscribed, she was frightened, for the loss of her father was still an unhealed wound. Yet she felt that each step took her closer to him, and closer to herself when she was small. Each step echoed many steps she had taken in years gone by.

When she found her father's grave, her heart leapt up in joy, as if she had climbed to the top of a mountain. It was a simple stone, shaped like an arch. She bent to lay the rose upon the grave. All at once the air was alive with an invisible wave of emotion, the feeling of something released. She knew her Treasure was near.

Looking up, she saw a stallion. He was running on the other side of the trees—a magnificent vision! She heard the snorting of his breath and the echo of his hoofbeats. She wanted to run to him, but before she could move...

21

He was gone.

Only one thing was certain. She had seen a horse. But was it Treasure? Or only the ghost of a memory?

Amanda knew she had changed a great deal in thirteen years. But the stallion was exactly as she had remembered him, as if he were frozen in time. Could he be waiting for her? Would they ride together ever again? Many questions came into her mind, but there was no one to answer them.

22

CHAPTER FIVE

FORTUNE

O n the other side of the mountains was a city by the sea. She had heard there was a house of fortune there. She had been told that the house was special, a place where you could ask strange questions and where you might be given answers.

It was still light when Amanda arrived. Much to her surprise, she easily found the house of fortune. It was guarded by two stone lions. Above them a light shone in the window against the coming night, and the front door was open to all seekers. The lions made her uneasy. Their stony snarls reminded her of the stones in the cemetery. But her own confusion, and the mystery of her missing Treasure, frightened her even more. She stepped across the threshold.

At the end of a long hallway were narrow stairs that led to the room with the beckoning light. Amanda would come to learn that in each town where people lived there was always a house with an open door and a light in the window above. And though there were many such houses in many cities and towns, they all led to the same room, the room she now entered.

Amanda was surprised by the nature of the light. Although night had fallen, the light in the room remained a little like dusk, a little like dawn. She couldn't tell which, or what would come next.

Near the door she found a green felt table. On it lay instruments of luck and fate: a pair of black dice; three small, delicate bones; and three coins of ancient age. She picked up one of the coins. It was larger than the others, and worn by a million seeking hands. When she turned it over, she found pictures of twelve tiny animals around the rim. One of them was a horse.

Against the wall stood an ancient fortune-telling machine. Inside its glass case sat a gypsy grandmother, made of wax, with lace-sleeved hands poised over curled cards. When Amanda approached, the machine whirled to life, and hidden gears guided mechanical hands in search of fate. *But this is not what I came for,* she thought.

"And what *did* you come for," asked a kind voice.

Amanda turned and was surprised to find a woman with clear eyes and strong hands, sitting at a second table of green felt. Her dress was also lace-sleeved, but this woman was real.

"I'm looking for my Treasure," said Amanda, as if it were obvious.

"Ah," replied the woman. "You can't expect to find him right away. It's one step at a time. And you must collect all the clues."

"Clues?" said Amanda. "How do I find clues?"

"You find them by taking The Journey."

Amanda was already tired from her day's travel, and she certainly didn't feel like traveling anymore. Reluctantly she asked, "How do I start The Journey?"

"You must have started already," said the woman, "or you wouldn't be here."

25

"All I want is to find my horse," mumbled Amanda. She was sleepy now, and she looked around for a place to rest her head.

"Then beware the man who is also a bird."

"What?" said Amanda, suddenly wide-awake.

"Oh, yes," warned the woman. "He will try to lead you away from where you want to go. He will lie with the truth, and make the true seem false. Though the path is simple, it is well concealed."

Without another word, the woman pulled a pack of cards from a green pouch and dealt seven of them onto the table in front of Amanda.

The first card had a picture of a king dressed in royal cloth. He was seated firmly on his throne, although from the dealer's point of view, he was upside down. The second had a frightening skeleton. The third had six empty cups and felt lonely indeed. The fourth showed a red devil with a pitchfork. Next to him a woman grieved and hid her eyes. *That's no way to find clues,* thought Amanda.

The fifth card showed a man serenading a woman beneath the moon, and Amanda felt better about that. But in the sixth, a man fell past a turning waterwheel, while a goddess looked the other way. The sun rose in the seventh card and drenched the world in light.

There was an eighth card, with a man on a horse. But the woman slipped it back into the deck before Amanda could look at it. Seven cards were all a person was allowed.

"What do I do now?" the girl asked.

26

"Each card is a door," said the woman. "I have dealt, but you must choose."

The girl did not know which card to pick. She passed her hand from one to the next. The light in the room seemed to change with each possible choice. Finally Amanda chose the card with the wheel that turned and the man that fell.

The woman said not a word more. She merely smiled her acceptance and closed her eyes. Whatever had happened, it was over now. Amanda felt she should leave. Clutching her card to her breast, she hurried from the room. The door immediately closed behind her.

In the room, the six cards remained on the table. Until a hand in a black glove scooped them up and put them back into the deck.

27

28

CHAPTER SIX

FISH

Returning to the street, Amanda felt like a mermaid out of water. She knew nobody in the city. She wanted to go to sleep, but she had no place to go.

She wandered along the cobblestone streets and recalled all that had happened to her that day. Suddenly the street ended, and for the first time she found herself at the edge of the sea. But it was not the vast, open sea her father had described to her so many years ago. This sea formed a bay. Thousands of houses, shops, and docks huddled around its rim, their twinkling reflections dancing on the water, as if it were a bowl and they were tiny fireflies drinking from it.

Amanda shivered as a chilling mist stole across the waves. She had no heavy coat to guard against the cool night air, and she was anxious to find a warm place to rest. She wandered until she heard the sound of a flute drifting through the darkness, a sonorous, country sound that was soothing to her ear. She turned and saw a small shop, but when she followed the sound through its bamboo doors she found...

It was not a shop at all. It was a tiny restaurant, paneled in exotic blond woods and painted with a blue wave that rolled across the walls. Diners sat in a row at the bar. They all seemed caught up in animated conversation as they

29

busily worked their chopsticks. Before them stood a fierce Oriental chef, dressed in white and wearing the thickest glasses she had ever seen. He waved her toward an empty chair.

She didn't know whether to leave or to obey. However, he seemed so certain of what she should do that she followed his direction. When she sat down before him, he swung a huge wet knife quickly through the air. Before she could move, he slashed a small fish to pieces. He deftly arranged the pieces on pillows of rice and offered them to her on a wooden tray. Raw.

She was embarrassed and wanted to leave. But just when she was ready to go, she remembered what the dealer of cards had told her. Clues could be anywhere. Even here. She had no choice if she wanted to find Treasure. So she stayed. But she could not bring herself to eat the raw fish. She slowly shook her head *no* and looked up into the chef's eyes, made huge by the thick lenses. The chef stared at her. Then understanding crossed his face. He sliced a multitude of fruits and arranged them like a miniature garden. He crowned the garden with a cherry and presented it with a bow. This she could eat and gratefully did.

Soon the other customers began to leave. But Amanda was not ready to wander the cold, misty streets around the bay again. She sat until the bar was dark and empty—even the chef had left—and the only noises were the crooning foghorns and muted sounds of the sleeping city. Then, from the rear of the darkened room, she heard the flute calling to her again.

This time it came from the kitchen, which still glowed with light. She peeked over a wooden screen and saw what must have been the chef's wife, dressed in a formal red kimono. The woman sat at a table under a brass lantern. She painted giant black letters on parchment with a brush.

Amanda could not understand the writing, but the characters were beautifully formed. She wondered if they might be a clue and wished she had something to copy them on. Tomorrow, she decided, she would buy a book and begin to record all the strange things she was seeing.

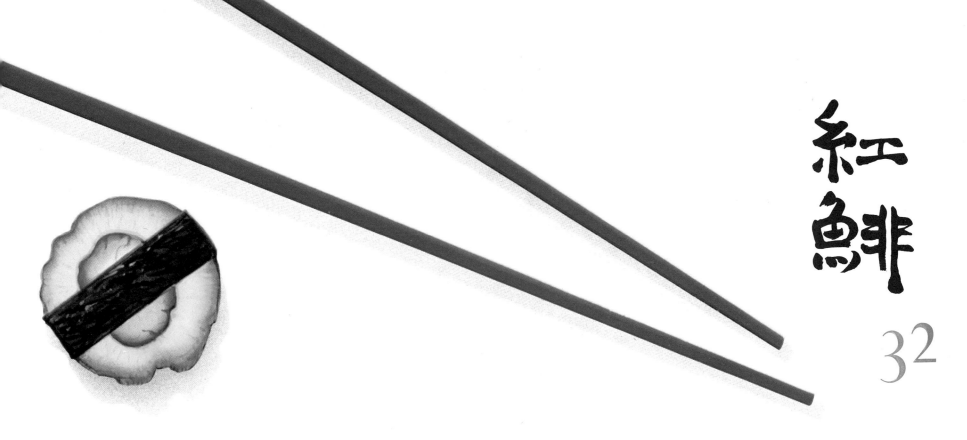

紅
鯡

CHAPTER SEVEN

ROAD

nchanted with the city, Amanda combed it endlessly for clues. But as week after week went by, the enchantment waned. Soon she began to feel awash in the babel of crowds and cars and to feel trapped in air so hazy she could barely see through it.

Now she had a book and carried it with her everywhere. It was bound in maroon leather and had thick paper pages, on which she wrote every important thing that she saw. Any sign of a horse. Any coincidence or paradox. Any puzzling thing. All were recorded in the book.

Every night, as Amanda sat in her room at the inn, she looked back over what she had written. She noticed that she had begun to write more and more about The Journey, and where it might lead her. She was beginning to understand that it was up to her to find a path. If she chose this fork, or that turn, it could take her in any direction. It was a matter of choosing the *right* direction, and more and more she felt that the right direction was away from the city.

But without her stallion to carry her away, The Journey seemed impossible. Then she found the car. It was older than she, sparkling white and in perfect condition. On its grille, leading the way, was the figure of a running horse.

She hesitated, unsure of what to do. She looked inside and saw the note on the driver's seat. It read, *Start me to your Journey's End.* She sat behind the wheel and turned the key, and it was like opening a door. On one side of the door was

the city and all her failures. On the other side was...the road.

The road was a landscape unlike any other, a blend of wind and clouds and the sun flashing through passing trees. It was a landscape of constant change, as if the road were flowing through her, and she flying above it.

The road led her along the glimmering ocean, past plunging seabirds, and into the night. It took her inland, through many small towns. She stopped in each town and described her lost horse. No one thought it strange, and they took the time to listen, to think, and to tell her what they had heard.

34

Many times she heard the rumor of a phantom horse. It roamed somewhere to the east, they told her in one small village. A magnificent Arabian stallion, they told her in another. In a third town some said the stallion had lost his master. Then she heard the stallion lived alone in the desert, drawn to the heat and sand by a thousand years of blood memory.

She stopped to buy apples from an old man at the side of the road, and he told her about an old Indian corral on the edge of the desert. A horse was sometimes seen there, a stallion. He came to the corral, the story went, looking for his missing master, the master he still loved.

She knew the stallion was her Treasure.

The air turned hot as she drove eastward. Unlike the city, here it was dry and clear with sunrises that were violent in color. She had been told the corral was invisible from the road. So she turned onto an unmarked trail and followed dusty, rutted tracks leading to the edge of the desert. And there it was.

The car's engine sputtered to a stop. Amanda felt a strange presence in the air, like silent thunder. She was certain Treasure was there. The corral had been formed of weathered split-rails in the shape of a figure eight, with an extra circle in its center. She ran to the fence and climbed up to see into the corral.

It was empty. She hurried to the gate, unlatched the rusty chain, and entered the corral itself. She turned and looked for life of any kind. But there was nothing.

She knew she should wait for him to come to her, but she could not. Her eyes caught the line of a great black bird that circled and soared above her. In desperation, she followed his shadow into the shimmering desert.

CHAPTER EIGHT

WILDERNESS

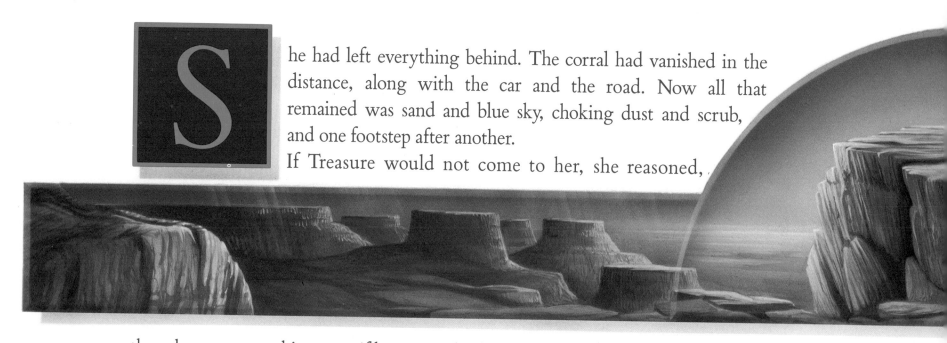

She had left everything behind. The corral had vanished in the distance, along with the car and the road. Now all that remained was sand and blue sky, choking dust and scrub, and one footstep after another.

If Treasure would not come to her, she reasoned,

then she must go to him, even if he was in the desert. But she could not feel him anywhere near. She only felt the weight of the sky pressing her down and the wind blistering her face.

It was the wind that chased her across hills and made her hide in the hollows to escape the stinging spray of loose sand. It wrapped her dress around her legs and made her wish for the comfortable green cape she had left behind.

Everywhere she looked there were footprints. But they were all her own. She could not retrace her steps, as she no longer knew the way she had come.

Sand gave way to rock, and Amanda started to run. Holding her book tightly, she ran with a springing step and a feeling that was somewhere between panic and joy. Around her now were puzzling rocks, huge granite mushrooms that towered above her. She imagined that she was Medusa in a giant garden and that she had turned it all to stone. Now she was the only life there.

It became too steep to run, and she began to climb. The stone that had looked rounded and smooth from a distance was actually sharp-edged and hurt her hands. The emptiness around her numbed her mind, and so she fixed her gaze on the highest point she could see. She no longer looked to the right or the left. All she did was climb...without thought of horse or clue.

At last she could climb no more. She was on a tiny plateau, an island in the sky. Around her were great primeval monuments, sculpted from the earth over thousands of millennia, and beyond them the wilderness went on forever.

As darkness fell, she looked back the way she had come. At the edge of the desert she could see tiny pinpoints of light. Although she was hungry and thirsty, and her hands were tired and raw, she was greatly relieved to see there was a beacon to guide her. And now she knew that she could no longer take The Journey without some kind of map.

38

CHAPTER NINE

MR. MAPS

The town at the edge of the desert, like an oasis, had grown around springs of water that bubbled from the heart of the earth. Here groves of plants and trees flourished. In this town was a keeper of maps. The innkeeper's wife told Amanda about him. He lived in a tiny house behind a grove of bamboo and far from the main road. By the time she found it, night had once again fallen.

His house was very odd, with the blinds all pulled down, and who was to say what he was like? Amanda was hesitant to ask the man for help, but she had come this far. She could go a little farther. In fact, the door cracked open before she could even knock. A wizened old man, who did not come up to her chin, stared at her with extraordinary blue eyes. He knew immediately what she wanted.

"Lost?"

He did not wait for an answer. The door opened wide and she saw an amazing collection of maps. Black and white maps, color maps, maps of states and streets and counties and cities. Maps of mountains and maps of valleys. Maps of every American place, and even of the sky. Maps, mostly old, with curling edges and finely drawn lines.

Maps filled the little house to overflowing. There were maps in boxes, maps in baskets, maps on the walls, and maps on the ceiling. (And even, she thought for a moment, maps floating loose in the air.)

"Lots of people lost nowadays," said Mr. Maps, stepping back to let her in. "Can't find the places they're looking for." Amanda said nothing, but it didn't matter. Mr. Maps was used to talking to himself.

"You gotta have a map." He admired his collection with obvious satisfaction. "Any place you want to go, gotta have one. 'Course the thing is" he turned to her whispering in a low voice reserved for secrets, "you got to know where you're going."

"Lots of places. Oh, my, lots of places you could go. But I got the maps for all of them." He opened a trunk to show her even more. But lying in the trunk on a pile of maps was a black falcon. Amanda couldn't tell whether it was alive or just a statue. "Yes, ma'am, can't have too many maps," said Mr. Maps. He hopped around trying to distract her as he hastily covered the dingus with even more maps and slammed shut the trunk. " 'Cause you never know what place you're gonna have to find."

"I got all these degrees and meridians...south of east...north of west...any direction you want to go." Any direction she wanted to go? She'd come all this way hoping the funny old man would tell her the direction she should take, and now he expected *her* to know where she was going. She felt so confused that the room started to spin. She and Mr. Maps turned into a globe, revolving like a planet lost forever among the stars.

41

"Take these maps," he said. "Trust me. You'll find what you're lookin' for." Amanda realized it was time to leave. She took the maps from his hands. And as she stepped outside, she turned to stare one last time into his enormous blue eyes.

Before Mr. Maps could say "Good luck," three maps darted through his doorway and escaped into the night.

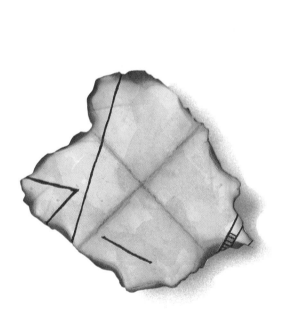

42

CHAPTER TEN

THE SIGNAL

All traces of a trail had been washed away with the first storm of the season. The raging ocean had raked clean the beach, then scattered it with objects from the bottom of the sea. Amanda found starfish and sea horses and the rusty skeletons of dead boats.

She had felt a little lost since abandoning the car at the edge of the desert, tired from constant walking and uncertain whether she would have a roof over her head tonight. Yet there was something comforting about this place. The ocean was unlike any she had seen before. This was the kind of sea her father had told her about when she was young. It had crashing waves and wide, sandy beaches. It was exactly like the place she had dreamt of long ago.

A signal rose out of the soft sea mist like a marker, bold against the sky. But when she reached the signal, the keeper's house was abandoned, a windowless, empty husk. So she crossed to the signal tower itself.

It was unlocked. The giant doors swung open with a scrape, and the sound echoed in the emptiness. Once inside, she found the place to be more complex than she expected. She could not go directly up the stairs. She had to go around a circu-

44

lar hallway. Only then, as if voyaging through a chambered nautilus, could she find the delicate spiral upward. One step at a time, she climbed toward a glow that drifted down from an opening above her.

When at last she climbed through the opening, she was suddenly bombarded by the dazzle of lenses. Light flashed and bent about her. Everything twisted and became too big or too small. Things came constantly apart, then together again, but in the wrong way. And although it was no longer attended, the signal continued to turn and to send out its light.

It was a shell of past intentions.

Amanda escaped to the windy balcony. She clasped the railing and tried to bring her feelings to a focus. The crashing of breakers and the cry of cormorants reached her ears. She looked out at the golden mist that ran from the sea to the cliffs and past the cliffs to the forest. Somewhere far beyond was the place where this had all begun.

Empty as it was, the signal was full of promise. For now she could see a great distance, and in many directions.

45

CHAPTER ELEVEN

CAROUSEL

The seasons were changing. Amanda felt herself running out of time, and hoped she would soon find her Treasure or at least another clue. Finally, in the last hour of an autumn night, she discovered a place she recognized from childhood. It had been a park when she was young, full of open green spaces and bounded by sturdy maples. It had been a place to play and let feelings run free. Now the land was the foundation for many tall buildings. The few maple trees that remained were on fire with the season, glowing orange and red under the late-night glare of city street lamps. But between the buildings, at the very center of what had been the park, she discovered long-remembered shapes still waiting in the dark. Shapes with arching necks and proud tails, shapes with wild eyes reflecting glints of light.

This was the old park carousel. And its horses, carved by hand a hundred years ago, were still there. Stepping onto the old wooden platform just before dawn was like stepping into a dream. She was surrounded by horses sleeping in the shadows. But where was her horse, the one she rode on Saturday afternoons, the one that looked like Treasure?

When she found him, she saw that his wood was cracked and his right eye chipped. His reins and stirrups were gone. Still, Amanda felt good to see him

46

again. She mounted him easily and warmed his cold brass with her hands, willing him back to life. As she sat there, something eerie began to happen. With a curious creak, sleeping cogs began to turn, to mesh and mesh again. The carousel slowly, ever so slowly, started to move. The horses began to rise, the lights to shine, and the years, one by one, to fall away.

As the carousel spun faster and faster, its organ began playing a familiar tune. When she looked behind her, she was amazed to see that the horses now had riders, and all of them were little girls, just like herself. She recognized no face, but she knew she was one of them, clutching old leather reins and the slick, stiff, arching mane.

Now the ticket taker came aboard. Silently he stepped from horse to horse, collecting pasteboard passes with each black glove. For he must always be paid.

The sun was rising. Its rays made the jeweled saddles gleam and the circus colors sing. In that early light, Amanda could see many romantic landscapes painted on the carousel, and of them all, only one called out to her. She recognized that it was more than just an ideal. It was a real place, waiting for her.

A place of living rock and snow.

47

CHAPTER TWELVE

MOUNTAIN

Entering the mountain domain, she discovered a different world. It was a world of frozen forests buried under ice. Of great glistening snow fields that stretched farther than the eye could see. Of a sky that was always near. It was a world of intimate distances.

The mountain was more beautiful than any place Amanda had ever seen. And it was more dangerous, too, for this was a kingdom ruled by the cold.

The cold was an invisible beast that stung her and cut her with each step she took. Nothing might move on this high mountain, the cold had decreed. It had bent over the green trees with heavy, hanging ice. And glazed the snow with a sharp and cutting crust.

Into this fierce realm came Amanda, inexperienced and unprepared. The cold sliced easily through her cape and soon had numbed her skin, her flesh, her bone.

Yet it was shivers of excitement that shook Amanda now. For the cold had swept the mountain air clear. All barriers were gone. She could feel her stallion's presence. He was close, nearer than ever before.

He appeared without warning, standing high above her on a great snowy ridge. His magnificent form was outlined against the white mountain peak. He

was calm, as if watching her, even waiting for her.

With her first rushing steps toward him, she stumbled and fell through the crust and into the deep, powdery snow. When she struggled to her feet, he was gone.

Now the wind sang a dangerous song, and the sky turned from gray to an ominous black. She knew she must reach shelter and a degree of safety soon.

Wading through the deep snow, she saw a dark shape at the timberline, sheltered by a bowl of rocks. Lights twinkled in windows there, and smoke rose from a chimney. It was a lodge, and she struggled toward it as fast as she could. Past that, she knew, lay only ice and dark, descending clouds.

The huge oak door to the lodge had already been barred for the winter. She could only bang the frozen iron knocker and hope that someone would hear her.

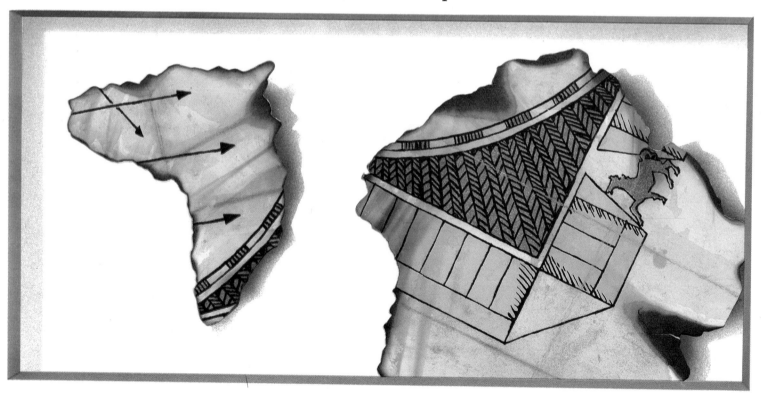

CHAPTER THIRTEEN

LODGE

Snowy winds blew high on the mountain slope, but she was warm and safe.

The caretaker had heard her knock and let her in. He was a gentle old man and kind enough to give her a room for the winter. The room had a chair and a quilt-covered bed, and the window looked back the way she had come. Her tracks were covered now, but she remembered how far she had traveled in the last two years and where she had been.

Storm after storm swirled over the mountain and the lodge. Between the storms were cold, bright days. But she always stayed inside. She spent the time in her room, writing in her book or reading before the fire in the great central hall.

"Searches are not all searching," the caretaker told her. "After great risk must come rest." For many days Amanda was like one of the sleeping animals that had been carved into the woodwork of the lodge, curled up against winter's cold. She thought her thoughts and mended her clothes while the days flowed into weeks, and the weeks into months.

The caretaker was good enough to give her lodging, but he was not much company. He liked the solitude of his winter retreat and was always off tending to some private chore.

Amanda was free to do as she pleased and go where she wanted.

As the winter went on, the lodge seemed to invite exploration. It was built entirely from roughly hewn wood, with many levels and countless doors. Some doors had ancient symbols or Indian signs carefully carved into the grain. Others had been given an unbalanced shape or odd handle. Some she could open, some were locked, and some she could move only enough to glimpse a dark room beyond.

She mapped the lodge in her dreams as well. Once she dreamt she was looking through a crack between a door and its frame and saw a hallway she had never seen before. At its end stood Treasure. She woke and wandered through the dark lodge. She found the hallway she had seen in her dream. But the only sign of the stallion was a plain iron horseshoe nailed to a door.

She was ready to leave before the spring thaw. But she did not have to wait for the caretaker to unseal the lodge's huge front portal. She had found a different kind of door, and with it this rule:

The way to move forward is
sometimes to go back.

55

CHAPTER FOURTEEN

MEMORY

Her book was close by her side as she stepped across the threshold. The light of day dissolved behind her.

When Amanda's eyes grew used to the dimness, she saw a miraculous thing. Waiting in a great hall were all the moments that she thought she had left behind. All the objects were there, as were all her wishes and all her dreams. Everything was waiting in a jumble. And the strangest things were connected.

A cord of a compass was wrapped around a cavalry sword. A haunting fragrance drifted through an empty photo booth. Leaning against the booth was a brass-helmeted diving suit, draped with a blacksmith's leather apron. Next to that was a wooden plate with pieces of shrimp on rice.

There were horses everywhere, even the carousel horse she had ridden again last autumn. She walked past horses made of wood, drawn on paper, and modeled of clay. But there was no horse of flesh.

Along the wall were many doors. They were shut tight, and she could not bring herself to open them.

Behind one she heard a thunderstorm. Behind another a woman was crying. She passed these by, choosing instead to follow a tinkling melody.

The sound led her to a music box. She recognized it at once, for it had soothed her to sleep on many a scary night.

To be certain this was the one she remembered, she opened it and saw again, inside the lid, the figure of a woman attended by cherubs. Amanda had called her "The Queen" and had loved to look at her smooth face.

Amanda's eye caught other beloved objects, and each drew her farther back. She found postcards her uncle had sent from his selling trips, with pictures of ornate stairways, great hotels, geysers, and a touring car in front of a canyon. There was her first book, *Mickey Never Fails,* its cover warped by rain because she had forgotten to bring it indoors one day. Nearby she found her father's simple pocket watch, with its stained leather fob and cracked crystal, which he had left behind on his dresser tray.

Finally she came to a room that was filled with just her childhood. Here were all the playthings she had ever known. A raggedy doll with only one arm. A little dump truck with worn-away wheels. A cheap metal train, and tiny people who rode on it, with earnest expressions painted on their tiny faces. And in a far corner, at the back of a shelf, she found a wooden paddlewheeler with a waving American flag. She picked it up, and it felt good to have it in her hands again. For this was the boat on which she had taken her first imaginary journey in search of her missing Treasure.

CHAPTER FIFTEEN

RIVER

A puff of steam blew from the whistle as the paddle wheel pushed the giant boat down the mighty river. For more than a century this steamer had churned the broad waters, bringing people to their destinations along an ever-changing course.

High above the turning wheel, Amanda savored the warm breeze. She had taken this journey many times in her mind, but now she was actually on the river. The splashing of the paddles was a sweet sound to her ears. And sweeter still was the sight of the passing green levee and the small sleepy towns beyond it. These were places Treasure would like. He could be near any of them.

She wanted to ask the captain their location. The rules of the boat forbade it, but she stepped over the chain anyway, and climbed the stairs to find him. The captain sat in his chair in the steering house, gold braid adorning his shoulders and cap brim. He was concentrating on the course ahead.

She was just working up the courage to speak when the captain rang the ship's bell. Once. Twice.

Suddenly, the sound of a distant whinny drifted across the water. Amanda turned and saw her Treasure running along the shore, gaining on the boat with every stride. He was different somehow and more powerful than she had remembered. Easily he matched the speed of the stern-wheeler, and his hoofs beat a ghostly tattoo along the earthen bank. Then the stallion veered to the right, away from the river. The trees passed between them, and he disappeared again.

On the deck below her, a steam calliope began a wheezing tune. But the song was deep and blue, and the hands that played it were gloved in black.

The sun fell backward in time, draining the daylight from the sky. A city shaped like a crescent moon waited around the river's bend. The paddle-wheeler slowed as it glided toward the wharf. In the timeless orange twilight, stevedores yelled from the bank. Ropes were thrown and made fast. A plank became a bridge to the shore, and Amanda walked across it into the night of the ancient port of Old Orleans.

60

CHAPTER SIXTEEN

DIXIELAND

Pirates and runaways had once wandered the streets Amanda now walked. They had come from many places, and each had left his language and his mark. Now all ran together in a delicious gumbo of sight, smell, and sound.

It was a city of music, and in the Old Quarter a black-gloved hand wound an ancient turntable. A scratchy record started a clarinet's lonesome call. The music reached Amanda and beckoned her away from the river and down the back streets. She didn't know the way, but the music guided her steps.

Amanda followed the song into the heart of the Old Quarter. Here she found many hidden courtyards. They could be seen from the street through tall, iron-barred gates. Each courtyard kept a secret, for these were private places. Amanda knew she didn't belong there, and felt guilty even looking in. Yet there was something fascinating about them.

Once this had been a city of blacksmiths, and their art was seen in every balcony and courtyard gate. The girl wondered if her father's work was near. She looked into each place for some sign of his hand, a familiar pattern or an arabesque of iron that could be a signature. But nothing was familiar.

The music had grown stronger. Now it seemed to come from all directions at once, echoing down narrow streets and along alleys. She opened a slender gate guarding a passageway. As she did this, the record's song gave way to a truer current in the air. It was the same music, but clearer and closer to her heart. At the end of the passageway she saw another courtyard. It was lit with a single pool of light, and in the light sat an old black musician with a clarinet. It was he who played the night music.

She was drawn to him, but as she came closer, a second gate of iron suddenly appeared, sealing the way. It locked with a click and would not come undone. She pressed against the cold bars, like a child at a window. She wanted to talk to the musician and find out all he knew. But he was beyond her reach.

The old man played seven more notes and each went through her heart. Then he put the clarinet down and all was quiet, except for the sounds of a port town at night.

From her cheek fell three tears onto the floor of slate.

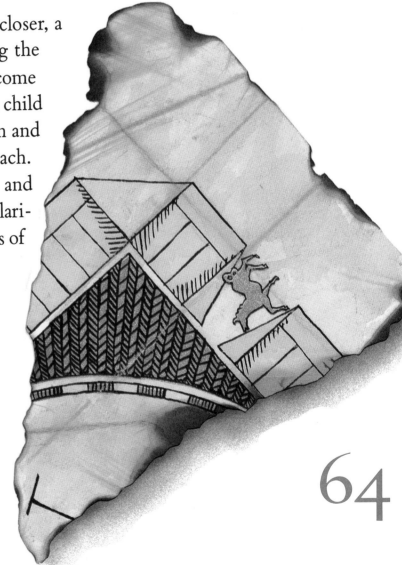

CHAPTER SEVENTEEN

FOREST

Early the next morning, Amanda left the city behind. She traveled the back roads, staying in country inns and keeping country hours. She saw each thing with fresh eyes, and if it caught her interest, she noted it clearly in her book.

The number of days devoted to her search no longer concerned Amanda. She accepted The Journey as her work. Each step was a step closer to Treasure. In this single-minded way, she moved forward.

One day she came upon an extraordinary forest, with trees of strange and wondrous shapes. It was surrounded by a ring of silence and stone. And though the morning was clear, the forest inside was dense with mist.

A tall stone archway marked the entrance. At its peak stood statues of animals, like sentries on alert. Each held a musical instrument, and when Amanda approached, the statues creaked to life, dancing a mechanical minuet.

The animals were charming, but like the trees, they were rather strange. *Well,* she realized, *I have become a collector of strange things.* And although the forest was obscured in the mist, she passed under the arch and entered.

Now things became curiouser and curiouser.

Amanda passed a lake whose surface reflected a castle. But when she looked up, she could see only clouds. Among the clouds sailed a big black hawk, which

let out a harsh screech. Nothing else seemed to move. There were only trees and statues of people. From a distance, the statues seemed frozen in time, but their faces were pitted and worn with age. The inscriptions carved along their bases were chiseled in strange languages she did not know.

It is as if everything is in code, she thought. *And I do not have the code book.*

Below one statue she found a book that might have helped. But it was written in the tongue of ancient Rome. So she copied only two short words and left the rest behind.

Now the mist became a thick white fog. *I'll never understand anything if I don't keep going,* Amanda thought, *even if I can't see where I am.*

Shapes soon appeared, and extraordinary shapes they were. There was a statue of a short man in a too-tall hat. Across from him was a rabbit, the handsomest she'd ever seen, well dressed in coat and vest. He held a watch with a fob. The watch was set precisely at eight.

The fog thinned even more, to reveal several cats and a caterpillar. And high above them all was the statue of a girl sitting on a mushroom. It was Alice from Wonderland.

Why, she looks exactly like me, thought Amanda. It was a comforting thought. For the first time she could remember, she didn't feel alone. But she did feel tired, for there had been a great deal to see and even more to think about.

I'll just rest for a minute, she told herself, as she joined Alice on the mushroom. On Alice's lap she put her book, and on the book she placed her head. Soon she began to dream.

66

CHAPTER EIGHTEEN

REHEARSAL

She dreamed at first only of The Journey and the places her feet had touched. Then, suddenly, she found herself peering into a room through a window.

Inside were two dancers, a man and a woman. Both stretched their legs on a long bar in front of a mirror the length of the room. She could see them. But they couldn't see her.

At the same time as she watched the dancers, her feet climbed a long and tortuous stairway. The stairway multiplied and became many stairs in many places, and her feet stepped from place to place. Though the stairs zigged this way and that, she was certain they led finally to her Treasure.

The dancers started a duet. The room grew huge, with hallways that stretched back for years. The man became the color of leather, while his partner in pink tried to twist and turn away. But no matter which way she danced, it was always into his arms.

The woman's hair was tightly wrapped in a knot when he lifted her up. But as he lowered her back down and bent her to the ground, her hair shook loose and curled in wanton ringlets around her neck.

Not right, Amanda said to herself. She was frightened at the way the dance was going. But it was beyond her control. She found herself stepping even more

67

quickly up and up the stairs. And worse, as the music rose to a climax, she herself became the ballerina.

Again he bent her to the ground, then raised her up and wrapped his arms all around her. And as Amanda fell back, she saw in the mirror the hands that held her.

They belonged to the Man with Black Gloves.

CHAPTER NINETEEN

PARTY

Amanda wrenched herself away from the dance and the stairs. She was determined to dream in a different direction. This time it would be her own.

In her second dream she knew she must talk to the rabbit.

It was a clear moonlit night. The rabbit's shadow moved across the window of a Victorian house on a hill. The house, she knew, had burned to the ground many years before. Why was it still standing, here, tonight? From inside came the sounds of a party. She tiptoed up the front steps and tried to peek through the windows, but they were frosted with fantastic shadows. She had no choice; to see inside, she must open the front door.

Inside the house, lit in eerie colors, was a bizarre costume ball. And the rooms were full of ghosts. They were dressed as pirates and policemen and ladies of the court. It was as if they were still alive, for they all wore masks that concealed their blank and staring eyes.

It was in this very house that they had been consumed. Caught up in the midst of revelry a century ago, they had ignored the smoke and fire. In flames they had been lost, and only on this night could they return to relive their end.

As if in a trance, Amanda moved through the crowded room. Indeed, it seemed she was the ghost, and they were the ones alive. Even worse, the Man

with Black Gloves had been here first and told them bad things about her. Naturally, she wasn't welcome. A tuxedo-clad man twirled an umbrella full of nonsense in her face. The others watched with dangerous smiles, and no one offered help.

But where is the rabbit? She had to find the rabbit. *Perhaps behind the locked door.*

She touched the door, which unlocked at once and revealed a dining room. She expected to find a banquet spread. Instead, the table was covered with masks. The ghosts had put them there for her to find. They wanted her to join them. But she was stronger now. She would do only what she wanted.

The rabbit appeared in the hallway, fascinated by the motion of a harem girl who wanted to dance for him. He would have followed the dancer away had not Amanda urgently tugged at his shoulder and refused to let him go. He was very large, and she had to stand on tiptoe to whisper in his ear.

"Where is my horse?" she asked.

"Here is a clue," the rabbit answered, "but I will mask it." Being late, he promptly disappeared. His gift remained in Amanda's hand. Though she did not yet understand, it was a card of many meanings.

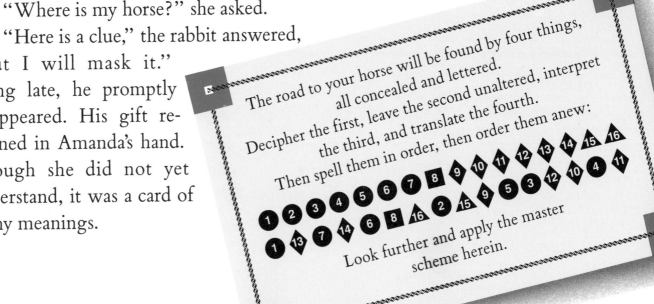

The road to your horse will be found by four things, all concealed and lettered. Decipher the first, leave the second unaltered, interpret the third, and translate the fourth. Then spell them in order, then order them anew: Look further and apply the master scheme herein.

CHAPTER TWENTY

COURTYARD

The night wind woke Amanda. She was exactly where she had fallen asleep: in Alice's lap, next to the tuxedo-clad rabbit. With her book she slid down to the ground and started to walk again. The night air was surprisingly warm.

She left the forest and headed toward a glow in the sky. It was the light of a nearby town, a place where travelers rested from their journeys. It appeared on every map, but not all who traveled could find it.

She had slept well into the night and when she arrived, the cobblestone streets were empty. On the edge of town, however, in a sweet-smelling grove of cypress, there was an old inn where the lamps still burned. Amanda followed the flickering flames to the center of a courtyard. A warm wind touched her cheek, and she felt strangely comfortable. She sat down at the first table she came to. A fountain bubbled nearby, casting reflected light across her table and onto the branches that hung above her. Along the far side of the courtyard, wooden fans whirled above an ancient bar.

She saw an old waiter leaning against the bar. He was dressed in a black vest and tie. He stayed where he was, patiently waiting. He seemed to have been waiting for her for many years.

"May I have some tea?" she asked. He bowed in answer and put a silver pot on a serving tray. But when he arrived at the table, she saw he had brought her a puzzling platter. It was certainly more than she had asked for. From the platter he gave her a red silk scarf, a fortune cookie and, at last, her tea.

She tried on the scarf, but the color was alarming. "This is much too angry a color for me," she said, and gave it back to him. The old waiter took the scarf, bowed again, and withdrew. As he walked away, she thought how much she liked his calm face and white hair. She cracked open the cookie and read the message: "THE MAP IS THE KEY IN MORE WAYS THAN ONE." *Oh,* she thought, *I have received someone else's fortune cookie by mistake.*

In the fountain cherubs rode copper dolphins that sprayed gentle jets of water into the pool. The murmuring of the water soothed her, and she opened her book to read. It told about the things she had seen and heard on The Journey, and about each clue she thought she had found. Going through the pages of her book in this peaceful place, she began to see how certain things paired with others. And how in all this there was a pattern.

The warm wind stirred again.

How little it takes to be happy, she thought. *If you know where to look, the path is always clearly marked.*

With that she took a pen and wrote just one last word. And she felt as if she had escaped from a box. No more would she search endlessly. Now she knew she would find what she had intended. And she closed her book forever.

In the morning, when the black bird flew overhead to find her, the book remained on the table like a ghost. But Amanda had left the courtyard. Never again would the black bird deceive her. The way could no longer be eclipsed.

She had learned the most difficult of secrets: how to see.

75

CHAPTER TWENTY-ONE

HORSE

Amanda followed a stream along the floor of the great forest. The giant trees swayed in the wind, and light fell over her like gentle leaves. The sound of many waterfalls urged her on. The years had covered the rocky hillside with fallen leaves and broken boughs of pine and fir. The leaves and boughs had decayed into rich soil, covered now by moss and fern that was soft beneath her feet.

Each step was a discovery. A piece of the final puzzle. A doorway in time.

A swaying bridge, built by hand from wood and rope, took her across a final chasm. As she crossed, the air became sweet with the smell of clover and hay. It was the early-summer smell of many years ago.

At the forest's edge she found an old barn. Plants had covered it in an innocent tangle of vines. But the big double doors still hung firm on their hinges. And on the doors, she saw handles of iron curled around in a curious design that quickened her heart.

It was his workshop. Her father's old place.

An owl startled her when she opened the doors. He circled the barn and perched on a nearby tree. He was the watchman who had watched through the night.

She stepped inside. Cool dust lay everywhere, for here time had truly stopped. Each article lay waiting as if its master would soon return. She found his anvil and hammer, the cold black furnace, and an iron melting spoon that was flecked with traces of gold. On the workbench lay her father's plaid coat. It was coarse to the touch, but when she picked it up and held it to her face, it felt warm and full of safety.

A chain lay on a clay sculpture of a horse. When she lifted off the chain and picked up the earthen figure she suddenly saw, pinned to the wall, drawings that had filled her dreams. They were swirling ink sketches of a spirited horse, his mane flying, his hoof pawing the air.

Through a dusty window, glass blurred with time, she saw a magical scene. In the meadow, waiting for her, was her stallion. He was where he had always been.

Amanda ran through the high grass to Treasure. She knew now that he was hers. He did not bolt but turned his head to meet her. And when she touched him, his skin glowed under her stroking hand, and he nuzzled her with his warm, velvet nose.

She felt her father nearby, as if she were a child again. But now she had grown tall, with strong legs and certain hands. Her fingers twined around Treasure's mane and she was on him in a second.

The wind brought the scent of the faraway sea. She could smell it and so could he. She talked to him with her hands and he understood. He turned with a touch and she guided him easily, for she knew the way. She had dreamt it often.

Amanda bent close to him, her hair mingling with his mane. This was the

way they rode all day until the waves broke at their feet and the sand flew high behind them. The sun slid down to the ocean. The moon rose, and still they went on together. For this was just their beginning.

And the horse of gold? Amanda did not need it. She had found her Treasure.

Now you find yours.

Take all the clues, hidden herein
Combine them and take their full measure
It's time for your search to begin
It may lead *you* to Treasure.

RULES

A sculpted horse made of pure gold and weighing 2.2046 lbs. (one kilogram) is buried somewhere in the continental United States. Within the belly of this gold horse is a compartment containing the key to a safe deposit box. Inside the safe deposit box is a certificate redeemable for $500,000 ($25,000 per year for 20 years.)

The object of this contest of skill is to find and recover the buried treasure based on clues as to its location. A complete set of clues— all the information needed to claim the treasure and the prize— appears in each of the following:

    1. The film "Treasure," available in a variety of formats, which include: videotape cassette, CED videodisc, and television broadcast of the program "Treasure."
    2. The book "Treasure" available at participating book retailers and book clubs.
    3. The interactive laser videodisc titled "Treasure."

WARNING—There are some points of information included in the above that could be construed as clues but are not. Additionally a degree of dramatic license has been taken.

Each of the complete sets of clues mentioned above has been constructed to lead to the location of the buried treasure. They may be considered different paths that lead to the same, exact spot in which the treasure is located. It is up to you, the contestant, to correctly identify those pieces of information which are genuine clues and those which are not. However, you may gain more information, and thus a greater advantage by examining more than one set of clues. You should not assume that information from one version can be applied to another version.

Additional information may be released by the sponsor and appear in various print, video, audio, electronic, and computer media which may be helpful in solving the "Treasure" puzzle, but this information will not contain a full set of clues and will not be necessary to find the buried treasure. To receive a listing of the specific media utilized for complete sets of clues and additional information, send a self-addressed, stamped envelope to: Treasure Request, P.O. Box 4249F, Blair, NE 68009. Available after July 31, 1987.

If the Gold Horse is not uncovered and the treasure is not claimed by midnight, May 26, 1989, the Gold Horse and the treasure will be awarded to one or more nationally recognized charities.

The Gold Horse was buried under the supervision of the D.L. Blair Corporation, an independent judging organization whose decisions are final in all matters relating to this contest. The D.L. Blair Corporation has verified that the puzzle is solvable in each medium where a complete set of clues is furnished (not in supplemental media where only additional information is furnished). Employees of Renan Productions, IntraVision, Vestron, Warner Books, the D.L. Blair Corporation, employees of all distributors of the program in any of its forms, employees of all affiliates, subsidiaries, distributors, advertising and promotion agencies, and the families of each, may not participate in this contest.

WARNING—ENTRANTS ARE ADVISED THAT THE GOLD HORSE IS NOT BURIED ON PRIVATELY OWNED PROPERTY OR IN ANY LOCATION WHERE TREASURE SEEKING WOULD REQUIRE DAMAGING ANY EDIFICE, CONSTRUCTION, STATUE, LAWN, GARDEN OR TREES. NO RESPONSIBILITY IS ASSUMED BY THE SPONSOR WITH REGARD TO ANY ACTIONS OR LAWSUITS BROUGHT AGAINST CONTEST ENTRANTS BY PUBLIC OR PRIVATE PROPERTY OWNERS.

No substitution of prize is permitted. Taxes on the treasure are the sole responsibility of the winner. This contest is void in the State of Vermont and wherever prohibited by law. All federal, state and local laws and regulations apply. The winner must agree to give permission to use his or her name and photograph to IntraVision for publicity purposes without any further compensation.

The name of the winner (or the charity or charities, receiving the prize) can be obtained by sending a stamped, self-addressed envelope to: Treasure Winner, P.O. Box 4582W, Blair, NE 68009. These requests will be fulfilled after December 1, 1989.